SEDUCTION IN SEDONA

BY
GIA WOLFE

Copyright © 2024 Gia Wolfe
All rights reserved.
No portion of this book may be reproduced in any form without written permission from the publisher or author except as permitted by U.S. copyright law.

In the distance, I can see a tall man walking in the haze of steamy heat rising from an asphalt road. His toned arms, chiseled features, and tan skin had my heart beating right out of my chest! As he approaches me, I can feel his eyes undressing me and I am reveling in it! I cannot wait for him to touch me and tell me that I am the only one for him. He looked at me with his green eyes, whispering "Time to wake up you're going to be late for work." Right about then the alarm goes off and I jump out of bed to get the day started. What a rude awakening!

Let's face facts. A busy businesswoman who is the boss in a male-dominated industry doesn't have a lot of time for romance. I don't have a lot of time to get my hair and nails done, but the more time I dedicate to my career the less time I have to dedicate to me as a woman. I live in Tampa Florida, am 35, single with no kids, and no real family or social life. I never thought I would ever find "The One". My name is Erica Hansen and I am a workaholic. There I said it.

The Monday after Thanksgiving was a beautiful day in Tampa. It was a windy cool day with a high of 70 degrees which is frigid by my standards. The sun was out, the sky was blue. Tampa is home to many waterways. The mix of old and new is everywhere you look. The old charm of Ybor City to the new River Walk is home to me. I love the warmth, vibrant colors, and culture that is Tampa Bay. It really was a picture-perfect day however; the office was already calling me with a crisis. I am a general manager for a developer. There are always fires to put out and some are literally...real fires. My boss is never in the office. He has developed much of the business district in the Tampa area and is well-known in the community. I have worked for him as a loyal and dedicated employee for over a decade. He calls me a real "ball buster", the label seemed to amuse him. I guess you have to be when you are dealing with this industry mainly of contractors who have little to no respect for a woman on the construction site. When I first started they would approach me and try to make small talk. Some would even get the guts to ask me out for a drink. I would not even give them the time of day. I am not interested in dating anyone I work with. I don't want to date somebody when I have seen their plumbers crack on a job site. I mean it's just not appealing. I have overheard all the trash talk about girlfriends or wives. Many of them fancy themselves as ladies' men or a damn cocksmith. I don't see them that way and certainly am not attracted to that type of man. I don't consider them my equal either. Not to sound conceited but they are not on my level spiritually, emotionally, or financially. I would always think of what my grandmother told me. "Don't be a nurse or a purse when it comes to men Erica."

I had made it into the office early and upon arrival my assistant Lisa advised me that the owner of the company wanted to see me in his office. I immediately thought something was wrong because he was always out on his boat. Lisa is the best assistant anyone could ask for and always has my back. She is a beautiful woman. Long brown hair, big almond dark brown eyes, tall with a willow-like frame, glowing smile, and complexion with the voice of an angel. The men in the office and contractors alike loved to stop by her desk even though she would not look twice at any one of them. Truth be told I think that is why many men like to stop and talk to her, they love the challenge of the unattainable woman. Lisa is happily married and a hopeless romantic. She was constantly advising me to get a life. She would always tell me there was more to life than this position and that my boss would replace me in a nanosecond with one of the many coworkers trying to claw their way up the corporate ladder.

My coffee is waiting for me with my daily schedule highlighted on my computer screen. Lisa asked me "How was your weekend Erica? Did you have a nice Thanksgiving?" I didn't do a single thing socially. My mind went to a flashback of me sitting on my couch indulging in pumpkin pie and not caring one bit about fitting into my jeans at that point in life. I had takeout delivered from a restaurant and stayed in my condo all weekend. I was productive and finished multiple reports. I answered, "I had a fantastic Thanksgiving Lisa, how was yours?" As she then began to talk about her holiday. I felt envious that she had children, a husband, and a real family life. Something I never experienced and could not even relate to. I was an only child. Both of my parents passed away in a car accident when I was only 19. I had no siblings and there was nobody left in my family. I didn't have cousins, both of my parents also came from a very small family. The whole idea of having a large family was appealing to me, especially around the holidays. I did enjoy hearing about Lisa's family life. I knew it brought her great joy. I could see her face light up every time she talked about her husband Tom. I wondered what it would be like to have a love like that.

My marriage fell apart 3 years ago. My ex-husband Marcus could never compete with my career and he knew it. I loved him, or at least I thought I did. Truthfully we were comfortable together but actually, I told, I was relieved when he asked for a divorce. When we got married we both decided that our careers would be most important and children were not a part of that picture. We wanted to travel and have a comfortable lifestyle. After a couple of years, he changed his mind and really wanted to have a son. It was not a part of my plan, especially at this point in my life. Marcus wanted it all including a family. The thought of that terrified me. My career was in full swing, at the time I wasn't even 30 yet. I didn't want to change diapers at all. Divorce was painful but I knew without question it was for the best. I had wondered if I blew my only chance at real love because I could not compromise.

Marcus met a much younger woman or should I say a girl just two months after we separated. In retrospect, I thought he may have known her before we separated although he completely denies it. She was only 20 years old at that time and stunningly beautiful, while Marcus was 12 years her senior. He could not even take her to a local pub when they met. She was not even the legal age to drink! A few months after our divorce was final they were married. They had a huge wedding at a very posh location in Tampa. I was happy for him but could not escape the sense of jealousy and resentment that he was able to move on with his life so seamlessly after our divorce.

The week after a holiday is always busy but Lisa and I figured out the plan for the day. I made my way upstairs to the owner of the company's office. His name was Montgomery James. He was a savvy businessman and even though I would never tell him this to his face he really is a genius. He was a very short man who smoked cigarettes. He had gray hair and dark skin and petite hands with hairy knuckles. The man had gray hair growing out of his tiny ears! Ugh! I wanted to contact his barber and tell him to remedy this look. I used to think he had to shop in the boys' department for his clothing. I always assumed it was because of his small stature, that he would overcompensate by being so aggressive in business. He was extremely ruthless and did not usually care much for sentiment, He was all business and as his General Manager, he expected the same from me. I started my career working for him as a young girl right out of college. He liked the fact that I got things done. I started out typing his memos and worked my way up to where I am now. He took a chance on me and it paid off for him in production and the fact my projects finished on time. He knew that I was a top producer and could mold others to do the same.

I sat down in front of his huge desk. He had this oversized furniture in his office and I could never understand why. To me it just made him look so small in this big leather chair. I made myself comfortable and looked towards the desk in front of me. It was the usual mess. Montgomery sits down and says "I noticed you finished and emailed all your reporting over the holiday weekend." I was feeling very efficient about producing this and thought he would love that I had completed a huge project. I replied eagerly "Yes, I finished and hopefully you will find the numbers and information that I provided sufficient." He looked at me and paused. He took a few moments to formulate his next sentence. "Erica, go on vacation. Book a trip. Do not hesitate. You have one week to book something and tell me where you will go. You must leave Florida. It's not a vacation if you stay here. You must leave your laptop behind and not complete any reports or respond to any calls or emails." I gulped, I felt panicked, confused, and intimidated and immediately felt my palms starting to sweat. I hadn't been on a real vacation in over a decade. I asked "Have I done something to make you angry with me? I don't understand! Why are you doing this to me? We have inspections scheduled and you are ready to break ground on the next project. You have never required me to go out of town to take time off. Why are you doing this now?" He responded in a gruff and dominant raspy voice "You are going to burn out. You will be no use to me if you are Ericia. I can't believe you worked over the Thanksgiving holiday from home! You need to do it before Christmas. Go have some fun and come back ready to work."

I left his office feeling overwhelmed. Where would I go right before Christmas? I didn't even have anybody to visit. I had no friends to visit for a staycation. All my friends were now married had families and were local to Florida. At one time Marcus and I had many friends that were also couples. We would meet them out for dinner and drinks while having the freedom to go for small trips around Florida. Now all my friends have children. Some have multiple children and have little time for anything else other than carpool lines and school lunches. Whenever I had called one of them to go shopping or have lunch they always seemed to have family commitments going on. Not a lot of time for shopping and lunch with me unless I was interested in them bringing along one of the kids. My whole life was this company and my position. My employees were a part of my extended family. I did keep them all at arm's length even Lisa, but they were all I had.

I got to my office and sat back in my chair. Lisa was not at her desk when I walked in but she made her way back from the copy room. She noticed me sitting at my desk with a stunned look on my face and asked me "Are you alright?" She made her way into my office looking very concerned. She sits down in the chair in front of my desk looking puzzled because I cannot even form words at this point. I then turn to her and say "Monty is demanding that I take a vacation. Now, right before Christmas when we have all this work to do and it's freaking me out." Lisa exclaims: "It's about damn time!"

Her joy had now irritated me. She is supposed to be on my side. Why is she happy about this? Is she trying to get rid of me? I asked her "Why are you so giddy about this" and her response was "You need to make time for yourself. Maybe you will find love" I erupt into laughter. "Are you insane? Of all people, you know that there is no time for that in my life. I think if I have to go on vacation I will go to a spa and try to relax." I watch my assistant leap out of her chair and sprint to her desk to grab her laptop. She is way more excited about this vacation than I am. I know at this point there is no sense in fighting with Monty or with Lisa on this so I begin to adjust to the idea. I know that when Montgomery speaks I must obey so I start thinking about destinations.

Lisa is busy typing away with a laser focus on her face. She says "Ooooh how about Europe? I could see you going to the Italian Riviera. That would be a blast, Erica!" I look at her, roll my eyes and say "No, not enough time for Europe." she then squeals "What about Hawaii?" I reject that idea "Too far for a week Lisa." She then says with a firm loud voice "Sedona!" I responded, "Arizona?" and she said "Yes! Beautiful scenery and Cowboys!" I chuckled. I could never picture myself going to that area coming from Florida but I felt that Montgomery and Lisa might be onto something. Maybe I do need a break and maybe going on vacation by myself would be relaxing and I could come back to my job refreshed and revitalized ready for work. I had never been out west so I was really intrigued by that idea.

Lisa had my itinerary booked before lunch. I had gone out to check on a job site and upon my return, my email was loaded with all the particulars. I knew I had a spa day lined up and a trip to the Grand Canyon on a train. She also reserved a rental car and told me to just "go with the flow". My flight was set and all I had to do now was pack my bags.

That evening I felt I had made a mistake. I went back to my condo, took a hot shower, and went to bed. That same night I had a dream, I never dream. I never remember my dreams but this time I did. I remembered seeing a man. A large man wearing a white cowboy hat. I got the sense that he and I were in a romantic relationship. I could not see his face or remember many other details. I did wake up feeling a bit aroused. As if I had an intimate encounter. I was feeling flushed and almost dare I say...satisfied? The next morning I thought it was weird that I booked a trip to Arizona and came home to dream about a cowboy. I didn't think much about it and went to work. I certainly did not want to mention this to Lisa. I would never mention that I had an erotic dream but the fact that I dreamt about a cowboy may have given her a reason to be ecstatic over my trip. I arrive at the office to find my assistant busy researching things for me to do when on my trip. I say to her "Lisa, please don't go too crazy here, check with me before making a commitment on something out of my comfort zone." She barely looks at me as she puts up her hand and laughs as she is laser-focused on her laptop.

A couple of days go by and I start buying clothes for Arizona. I have all my business clothes and nothing much for casual vacations. I decided to purchase a few designer jeans and a few sweaters. I was under the impression that the dessert was hot all the time but my efficient assistant Lisa informed me that the weather is chilly in Arizona after Thanksgiving and I may want to bring warm things. I was really clueless about what to expect and didn't really worry about it until the night before my trip. I could not sleep at all. I could only think "What have I gotten myself into?"

The day came for my departure. I woke up with high anxiety. I had not thought about this trip at all. I had left it up to Lisa to plan because in my position leaving for a week means there is a lot of work to do before going anywhere. Maybe that's why I never go anywhere because the work is tremendous before and after a trip. I opened up my email on my phone and found my itinerary from Lisa. All my ticket information and confirmation numbers for the car rental as well as hotel information. About the time that I was arriving to park my car in the airport parking garage and noticed that my ex Marcus was calling. I answer the phone only because he never calls me now unless there is a problem. I answered, "Hello Marcus, how are you?" He sounds a little anxious in his response, "Doing great Erica, I had to call you to give you some news before you hear from any of our mutual friends. I thought you should know that Amy and I are going to have a baby. We found out it's going to be a boy!" At that moment I am ashamed to say that my heart sank for a split second. I knew that it was what he always wanted. I had to respond with some kind of dignity "I am happy for you, I wish you nothing but the best Marcus, I have to go though because I need to catch a flight." He sounded stunned "Flight? Where are you going?" I laughed "I am going on vacation for the first time in years. I would love to tell you more about it but I really need to go. I think they are beginning to board the plane right now. Thank you for calling me to give me your big news. We will talk when I get back ok?" I hung up having so many emotions. I started to cry, I had feelings of regret, jealousy, and resentment. I began to second-guess my decision to divorce Marcus. Should I have agreed to have children? I then started to think about the journey I had planned with Lisa. As I looked at my phone, I realized that I had a new path laid out in front of me. I started to feel a sense of excitement and anticipation of new possibilities. I knew I would be going on an adventure but I had no idea how my life was about to change.

The flight was long and nonstop to Phoenix. I could not help but think about Marcus, his new wife, and the baby now on the way. I was emotional over the thought of him having a child and moving on with life without me. I fell asleep on the plane and had another strange dream that I could barely remember. All I could recall was that I felt happy and content. I could not understand why even with a short nap I was actually dreaming! Why is this happening to me all of a sudden? Is it due to the fact that I have left Tampa and I'm on my way to a place where I have never been before? I woke up in enough time to watch another plane landing on a runway not far away. It looked like we were landing in tandem. It was exciting to watch. I had not been out of Tampa in years. I could not help but feel I was ready to embark on a great adventure!

I got my rental car with no problems and started my GPS, location destination Sedona. The drive out of Phoenix was not a problem but once I started to get close to my destination it was terrifying! They were working on the roads and the mountainous terrain was treacherous. I was stopped by workers and there was at least a 400-foot drop on the side of the road. All I could see were the tops of huge trees. I could see my white knuckles on the steering wheel. I was sweating even though it was 48 degrees outside. I thought I would never make it there and contemplated turning the car around but there was no room for that on this two-lane road winding up this rock mountain. The road would have some areas that were not so dangerous but I was not accustomed to driving up a mountain. In some areas, they were working on the road so we had to be routed with workers in a route that hugged the shoulders of the road. I could barely breathe while driving in these areas. I thought I did well all things considered. After all, I didn't have a heart attack or need for a diaper on my way up and down the mountainside.

I arrived at the hotel. Never been so happy to have both feet on the ground in all my life. I felt like kissing the sidewalk after the drive-in but worried the hotel staff would think I was totally unhinged. I am afraid of heights so this area will be a major challenge when getting out of my comfort zone. Upon arriving I noticed the architecture because, after all, it's in my field of expertise. It is so different from Tampa. The colors in Arizona are beautiful. The rock monuments are stunning. The terracotta colors are prominent in everything you see. The blue sky against the red rock is breathtakingly beautiful. The air is dry and not at all like the sea breezes I am used to. The hotel is rustic. I noticed my hotel room had oversized leather furniture, large wood beams that stretched across the ceilings, and a large stone fireplace in the corner of the sitting room. The bedroom was adjoined and had a large log-style bed. It was tastefully decorated and much to my surprise quite comfortable. I shot Lisa a text message saying. "I got here safely, the hotel is beautiful. Is everything okay at the office?" her response "You're welcome, don't ask about work. You are on VACATION!" I respond with a meek "thank you for everything" and try to get organized and unpack. Even on vacation I am organized! Some would say OCD (obsessive-compulsive disorder).

I decided to do some sightseeing. I went to the front desk and asked the girls "This is my first time here. What would you recommend?" Well, they came up with quite a few options. They were very informative and knew the area really well. Lisa of course had some to-do's listed in my itinerary. I knew I had a spa visit scheduled for the next day. The girls at the hotel told me that Sedona had vortex locations. I know they are energy hubs. I also know that they can be a moving experience. I thought I would try to meditate and become more self-aware at specific vortex locations suggested by the girls." I was totally intrigued and could not wait to check out my first vortex!

I decided to make my way to Bell Rock formation. Lisa had talked about this place and had done some research as well as forwarded the location to my email so I decided to check it out. I drove there without much of a problem. When driving to this location you cannot help but notice all the glorious colors of the desert. The black top with the yellow stripe painted down the middle of it stands out amongst the artwork of the desert. The rock formations were like something you would see on another planet. I wondered how this happened in nature. Even though you learn of this through science class in school but to look at this in person one struggles to find the words. Someone can only wonder how this all came to be. Bell Rock had many visitors on the day of my visit. This rock formation does look just like a bell. The red rock stretched to the sky with multiple trails leading to the top. The top is actually flat. It seemed to be a hot spot for tourists. I realized that I was a tourist so I felt right at home taking pictures. I watched people hike a trail from the road. I thought if I am going to feel a vortex I may have to climb this rock formation. I never actually felt any kind of energy that the girls at the hotel were telling me about but I did enjoy the view. I hiked up the side of the formation for about an hour and then made my way back down. I was pretty exhausted, the most exercise I get is on my treadmill at home. The uphill climb tested my endurance. My legs were burning. The sun was very warm but the air was brisk. The air was noticeably drier than what I was used to. I was soaking it all in. The red gravel ground, the formation of Bell Rock towering above me. I did feel exhilarated but I didn't contribute the feeling to a vortex. I was just happy to be in Sedona.

 I went back to the hotel and decided to order room service. I took a hot bath and went to bed. I was totally exhausted. I slept like a baby and I didn't know if this was due to the hike on Bell Rock or the dry Arizona desert air. No matter what, I was happy to get the rest that I never seemed to get at home. I woke up at 4:00 am Arizona time.

I could not go back to sleep but I realized I had slept for 9 hours. I noticed that my pillow was wet. I thought how odd, why was it wet? Then I realized that I had such a deep and restful sleep that I actually drooled on my pillow. Could this actually be happening to me? Am I really that relaxed that I could drool while sleeping? How could this be? I knew I was well-rested and ready for the day. I decided to wear a new pair of jeans and a white sweater. I put on my new hiking boots and a cashmere coat. Then I decided to go to the Mesa Airport in Sedona. I heard from the girls at the hotel that this was a vortex. I was determined to feel what this vortex business was all about.

When I walked out of the hotel I noticed a dusting of snow was on the ground! I hadn't seen snow since I was a child on vacation with my parents. I decided to take a drive up the rock formation to a vortex location the girls had told me about. Again, I noticed my hands clutching the steering wheel as if my life depended on it. Just like the drive into Sedona the road to get to the Airport was just as dangerous. Steep inclines and deep drops on the road forced me to concentrate and focus on my driving. Once I reached the Airport site I walked around the very top by the helipad but was unable to really get a good view of the area below. The area was closed at this time of the day but I was determined not to waste this drive to the top. I was focused on getting a view of the canyon everybody was talking about below. I wanted to feel the vortex experience. I decided to go to the spot I scoped out on my way up. It seemed to have a few parking spots and there were no cars there on my way up so I decided to see if this would offer a view. I parked and hiked to an area where the view was breathtaking! The panoramic view of the canyon was unreal! I knew immediately this was a vortex. I sat down on a rock. It was smooth, red, and ice cold. I really didn't care about the cold or wet rock. I wanted to try to meditate and feel this vortex everybody was talking about. I started inhaling a deep breath and holding it while exhaling slowly. I was trying to clear my mind. I couldn't take my eyes off the canyon. The snow-tipped treetops against the red stone with all the colors of the rainbow glistening as the sun was rising. I found myself feeling electrified. It felt like my hair was standing up on the end! I thought there was static electricity in the air. I was feeling so alive and free. This overwhelming feeling of joy was washing over me. It was like nothing I had ever experienced before! I was not even cold!

While sitting there on the rock absorbing all the energy around me, I start to sense something strange. Was it the vortex everyone was telling me about? I then hear this panting and feel this licking on the back of my head. I shot up from the rock and stumbled falling to the ground. I was being assaulted by a labrador puppy about 5 months old. He was almost orange from the mixture of snow and gravel. He was so excited to see me but I didn't feel so excited to see him. I then felt something warm and wet on my leg. I look down to see that he is now peeing on my new jeans and hiking boots. Not because he was lifting a leg to mark his territory he was so happy to see me and so out of control he was peeing all over me! His tail was wagging and he actually looked like he was smiling. His tail was thumping on my leg as it wagged.

I never considered myself to be a dog person and I felt violated by this puppy. He had interrupted important personal growth and I was very annoyed at the piss on my leg! I then hear this deep voice yelling just down the path "Winston! Winston come here boy!" This dog is not paying any attention to the voice at all. Winston was more focused on me still wagging his tail and squirting all over the rock and my boots. From the path, a man with a white cowboy hat emerged. I gasped. At this point, Winston knew he was in a bit of trouble. He said firmly "WINSTON!" I watched as Winston stuck his tail right between his legs, put his head down, and started to timidly walk over to what I now knew was his master. I also watched the trail of pee dribble right over to this man who was not paying any attention to me as he was trying to put the collar back on his dog. At this point, I am enraged over my jeans and hiking boots getting christened by Winston not to mention the fact he ruined my meditation session. "Do you think you could keep your dog on a leash? Why would anybody let their dog run here? Are you crazy? Look what he did to my boots and jeans!" He responds with not much concern "Sorry he is just a puppy." I then say with clear disdain "CLEARLY, puppy or not he needs to learn some manners and maybe you should too!" He quips back "You're not a dog person are you?" Now mind you, I like animals just like the next person. If I had to choose a pet I would select a cat. They are not high maintenance. I was not amused and felt his question was dismissive and rude. The only thing I am thinking about at this point is how am I going to get my jeans and boots cleaned before going home. I certainly don't want to pack them in my suitcase. I then answer him back sharply "I like dogs that are well-behaved."

I could not help but take notice. He was wearing an old worn brown leather jacket, an aqua blue and white checked flannel shirt, and jeans that he filled out actually quite perfectly. He was very muscular with a dark complexion. This man had the greenest eyes I think I have ever seen. He had brown wavy hair cut short and a well-trimmed beard and mustache. I could smell his cologne. He smiled and tipped his hat and said "I am sorry about your jeans. He just got off his collar and ran off. I am really sorry Ma'am". He got the collar back on the dog, continued his way down the pathway, and disappeared from sight. I was speechless for the first time in my life. I didn't know if it was due to this magical place, or if it was this man I just encountered. Or maybe it was the dog that left me speechless. How could he just walk away after his dog pissed on me?

Me being OCD and not willing to go through the rest of my day with dog pee on my jeans I decided to make my way back to the hotel for a quick change. I thought I would grab some breakfast and then take in the spa treatments. So I too start making my way down the path behind them. I then say "That's it? No offer to pay for my shoes or jeans?" He doesn't even turn around. He chuckles and says "Lady. It's just pee. It will wash out of your jeans." I am now mad as hell with wet jeans on. Before I can say a single word I slip on a bit of slick rock that has a thin layer of ice and snow on it. I panic as I start to tumble down this pathway, grabbing him by the shoulder trying to hold my balance but rolling down the hill taking him and the dog with me. All three of us now roll about into a small clearing lined by smooth red rocks while Winston lets out a yelp. This man lands right on top of me! We look into each other's eyes for a split second. I again noticed the color of his aqua-green eyes that reminded me of the bay waters at home. He has chiseled features, with defined laugh lines although at this time he wasn't laughing. His facial hair was salt and pepper colored and trimmed. I could smell his cologne again which reminded me of patchouli but with a hint of musk that was so manly. I never smelled cologne like that before. As I was immersed in his scent he quickly turned to look for his dog. He bolts to stand up and begins to examine Winston while I sit there stunned on my ass. Winston is clearly fine as he lunges for me again. He is now on his collar and the man had a grip so he didn't get a chance to violate me again. At that point, I am totally covered in red gravel and dog pee. He looked back at me as if I were a total idiot frowning at me with a scowl. He did work up enough effort to ask me "Are you okay? You should be more careful, you could have hurt yourself or my dog." I am so embarrassed at how clumsy I was navigating down the slope and responding "I am FINE. I slipped and it was an accident!" He offers me his left hand to help me up and I refuse. I noticed he had a braided leather bracelet on with no wedding ring on. I stand on my own, pulling myself up by the large rock and brushing myself off. He now looks annoyed while brushing off his jeans and struggling to keep Winston in check. He turns back to look at me again and tips his hat while he then starts to head down the path.

    I follow behind at a safer distance this time. I knew my face was as red as the surrounding rocks. I was truly embarrassed but I was also insulted at the fact he was more concerned over his dog than me. I see him get into a white Ford F350. I fire up the engine of my little Kia Soul rental car and start my way down the road at a very slow pace. My grip on the steering wheel is tight and my knuckles are white while clutching the steering wheel. My palms are sweating because of the steep incline of the road. There are no hills where I am from, certainly no mountains! I now see in my rearview mirror the F350 coming up fast behind me. I cannot believe that he is starting to tailgate me. I think that he is totally insane to drive this way down the road that has this type of incline. I think this is local to the area because the roadway is not a challenge for him in his huge truck. At this point, I am having severe road rage. I am starting to sweat and feel palpitations. My palms were sweating and it was now hard to grip the steering wheel. How dare he? I mean his dog pissed on my leg and now he tailgates me down a 75-degree slope! I decided to take my time and not give in to his intimidation. He beeps his loud foghorn multiple times. I am now livid, all sense of embarrassment is totally gone and I am thinking that now he has gone too far. I then take my foot off the gas and start riding my brakes going even slower, about 20 mph in a 35 mph zone, not allowing him to pass me driving right down the middle of the road on a two-lane highway. As we wind down the mountainside we approach a stop light. I get in the right turn lane as he merges to go left. As he pulls up next to me I lower my window and extend my well-manicured middle finger. I saw his face for a split second with a look of shock, mouth hanging open as I drove off.

I got a good laugh as I drove away. I didn't want to spend the day in dirt and dog pee so I went back to the hotel to shower and change. I wanted to try to get breakfast before heading off to the spa for a relaxing time. I felt so stressed out after my encounter with Winston and the cowboy with the green eyes. I made a quick change and made arrangements for my clothes and shoes to be cleaned by the efficient staff at the hotel.

It was now about 8:30 am Sedona time. As I pulled out of the hotel parking lot I noticed on the horizon 5 hot air balloons drifting off in the Oak Creek area! This was an absolutely stunning sight to see even at a distance. I wanted to follow them in the worst way but even if I knew where they were going there would be no way to catch up to them. I could only watch them from a distance as I parked my car in a nearby lot to just look up at the sunlit horizon. Watching the multi-colored balloons float among the clouds in the distance. It was inspiring to see. I sat on my hood for about 15 minutes just to take it all in.

I wanted to check out a restaurant that was close to the downtown area. I decided to grab a bite to eat before my spa appointment. I popped into the cutest restaurant that had a modern southwestern vibe to it. The menu featured spicy type foods rich with the culture of the area. The breakfast was so delicious. I enjoyed an omelet with chorizo and peppers. It was almost like eating an enchilada with the most delicious cornbread I have ever had in my life. The Hopi, Navajo, and Tonto Apache Indian tribes to name a few had left an indelible footprint on this area. Signs of this were everywhere you looked. The buildings blended in with the mountainsides. Even the local McDonald's looked as if it belonged there. It surely didn't look like any Mickey D's you would see back home. It blended in with the mountain scenery. Nestled into the red rock it could not have been more perfect.

I made it to my scheduled appointment at the Mii Amo Spa, which is a desert oasis, located near the Bell Rock formation, and was just what the doctor ordered. Lisa booked a day retreat fit for a queen. I felt so pampered having a hot stone massage, facial, manicure, and pedicure. I noticed that I chipped a nail probably when trying to fight off the beast of a dog that assaulted me on the mountaintop by the airport. It was on the same finger I flipped off the cowboy with so I again felt justified in my rudeness. This retreat was precisely what I needed. I would never admit it to Monty. I realized that I needed this getaway and it really could not have been any more perfect. The perfect time and the perfect place. The treatments left me feeling relaxed, calm, and almost in a hypnotic trance-like state of mind. Even though it was fairly early in the evening in Sedona I decided to get take out and head back to my hotel room to get some rest.

I had no trouble falling asleep that night. I was so comfortable after my spa day that I dropped into a deep coma-like sleep within minutes after my head hit the pillow. That night while sleeping, I had a dream about the cowboy I met at the airport lookout. I remember him looking deep into my eyes, then taking my hand as we walked along a path that was lined with juniper and pear cacti. He is quite a bit taller than me and I fit very nicely under his arm as he pulled me into his side. Wrapping his muscular arm around my shoulders and squeezing me tightly. He leans in for the kiss and ....BOOM! I sit up in my bed as if I were having some kind of nightmare. I am not one to even remember a dream or a nightmare for that matter. I could not help but wonder how could I even think about this rude guy who lives over 2000 miles away from me. Even still, he was on my mind when trying to get back to sleep. I could not seem to think about anything other than him.

Sedona has many roundabouts. If you are not sure where you are going you can just keep going in a circle until you figure it out. I did that more times than I care to admit. The next day I decided to check out an area that had many shops and looked like it could have been there since the 1800's. The Tlaquepaque Shopping Village had it all. Unique shops with cobblestone paths, water fountains, art galleries, and restaurants. I wandered around in this place shopping, eating, and not really caring about the time. The architecture is so amazing. Not at all like Florida. I could not help myself. I ended up buying many souvenirs. I thought I would get a few things for Lisa and her family. I also purchased a few items that I knew would remind me of my time in Sedona.

I noticed a metaphysical shop across the street. I walked in and instantly felt at ease in my surroundings. There were many tourists there with the smell of incense permeating throughout the shop, and a small woman behind the counter smiled and welcomed me in. I looked through the glass countertop to see many pieces of jewelry that I felt were indigenous to the area. Some stones were mounted in a ring setting and others were in slide-type necklaces. I purchased a charm and a ring from the lady who welcomed me in. Another woman behind the counter asked, "Are you visiting our town for the first time?" I smiled and nodded "Why yes I am. Do I look like a tourist?" She giggled with a glint in her eye and said "Yes ma'am you sure do." She asked, "Where are you from somewhere warm I think right?" I quickly replied back "Tampa Florida" She looked as if she knew the answer already so I asked her "Don't see many people from Florida around here?" She replied "We get them from all over. Oh, I feel you met one of our locals?"

My head snaps back around and I quip "Excuse me?" Again this woman is giggling and I am not sure why. Do I have something on my face? Do I have toilet paper stuck to my shoe? I think to myself what is so damn funny? This woman is about 70 years old, small frame, very dark, and weathered skin. I thought she was Native American but I really couldn't be sure. Whenever she looks at me she seems to be amused. I then ask her "Why are you laughing at me?" With a loving smile, she reached out for my hand. I give her mine and look into her brown eyes. She closed her eyes as she cupped my hand in her petite little hand. She took a deep breath in and said "My dear, I am not laughing at you. I know you just met the love of your life while here on vacation and I have to admire your gumption!" I immediately snap my hand back and start to think she is out in left field. There is no way that the man I met yesterday, actually the only man I met, or kind of met yesterday is the one for me. "No ma'am, I didn't meet anybody yesterday, especially not anybody to fall in love with." As she responded back to me with an even bigger smile, "We'll see."

I left the shop now feeling a bit uncomfortable. How did this woman know that I met somebody yesterday? She seemed so sure of herself when she told me I met the love of my life. How could she possibly know that? I know the area has many spiritualists. Many of the shops have psychic readers waiting to just take your money. I have never had a lot of faith in any of it. I thought they were just out to scam anybody they could out of their hard-earned money. I didn't think there was any truth to this kind of nonsense. Even still, I couldn't help but wonder what she was talking about. Who was she? How does she get this knowledge?

I continued to walk around the shopping area. I was beginning to buy many things and bring them back to the little rental car I had. I found quite a few pieces for my apartment that I thought would not travel well. I bought some crystals and an intricate lamp so I decided I would send it back home through the mail. I wanted to pack it with bubble wrap to ensure it got to my office in one piece. I could not imagine taking this on a plane. I went to the Post Office in Sedona. I was struggling to wrap the lamp out of the trunk of the rental car. I had bought all I needed, the box, wrap, and tape per US Postal standards. I was not used to doing this kind of thing. This was something Lisa would always do for me in the most efficient way. Here I am struggling to address the address label.

Out of the corner of my eye, I see a white truck pull into the spot 2 spaces to my right. As it passes me I see it's the cowboy with green eyes. I freeze for a second in fear. At that time I was not sure if I should fight or flight. Do I run off and leave? I was hoping that he didn't recognize me or the rental car and I continued to focus on my package by trying to wrap tape around the box. I am almost sitting inside this small trunk hoping not to be noticed.

I see him walking up to the post office door while looking through the window of my car, he stops on the sidewalk, and squints while removing his aviator sunglasses as he looks my way. I feel a bit of energy surrounding me and a pit in my stomach that I had never ever felt before. He is wearing the same white cowboy hat and this time he had on a red flannel shirt and jean jacket. I see the scowl and look of disgust, I know he recognized the car and I can clearly see the frown on his face. I watched him as he bent down slightly to look into my window as he continued to pause to look my way. He then continued into the Post Office. I contemplated leaving as quickly as I possibly could. Then at that moment, I realized that I was not my usual self. I remembered that I am a savvy, confident businesswoman who can make my own way in this world. I had never been intimidated by any man before and this was no time to start. I finished putting the tape on my oversized box, grabbed the box along with my handbag and keys, and shut the trunk. I refused to be intimidated, I was mailing this package off today!

I walk into the small post office and I immediately notice him standing in line. His piercing eyes look at me as I walk in struggling with my large box. I am next in line behind him so I put the box down in between us. There are 4 people ahead of us and one postal worker in this tiny waiting area. I noticed the smell of his cologne again. It's the same scent that he had on the other day. I have a hard time trying to focus on anything. The air seems as if it is full of static electricity as my palms begin to sweat. I snap back to reality and I begin to remember how he was laying on his horn the last time I saw him driving down the mountain. I tried to remember my road rage but it was difficult and I couldn't figure out why.

He looks my way with a smirk "Good morning." I roll my eyes, almost disarmed. "Morning." The line begins to move at a snail's pace. I slide the box on the floor with my foot. The postal worker is slow but seems to know everybody's name. She greeted the last two customers by name so I could not wait to hear what his name was. I noticed his body filling out his jeans. Most men wear jeans that are baggy these days but not this cowboy. His Levis were snug on his legs and ass. He glanced my way several times as we waited in line. After standing in line for several minutes it was finally his turn. The teller's face lit up like a Christmas tree, smiling a toothy grin with delight "Good morning Austin! How are you today?" He walks up to the counter and smiles back at her, "Just fine today Mrs. Perry, How are you doing today? How is the family?" "Oh, they are just fine. Do you need stamps?" I watch as they exchange niceties. They have obviously known each other for years. His name fits, he definitely looks like an Austin. Mrs. Perry takes care of his postal needs and I catch her saying "Give my best to your daddy Austin." He smiles and tips his hat at her 'Yes ma'am.' and then looking back at me does the same hat thing with a half smile and says "Ma'am." as I watch him walk out the automatic door.

I still smell his cologne lingering in the air when I walk up to the window as Mrs. Perry greets me with a smile "Can I help you miss?" I put the box on the counter. I tell her about my great finds and how I need to send it back home so it won't get broken. She clearly agrees that this is a smart move. She then asks me "Do you live in Tampa? I have never been to Florida before. I bet it's beautiful." It was very easy to chat with her. She looked like somebody's grandmother. White hair, glasses, very short with a warm smile and kind eyes. Nobody was behind me so I felt it safe to confide in her about my encounter with Austin.

"Mrs. Perry, how well do you know that man who was in line before me, Austin?" she responds "Oh my, I have known that boy all his life. His family owned a large strip of stores downtown for years. He's a good boy, Do you know him?" Not really knowing if I should admit to the middle finger incident I shrugged. I responded, "I thought he looked familiar but I don't think I know him at all." I could not help but wonder about him. Did she know this man since childhood? "Mrs. Perry shakes her head "He's a kind and good-hearted man" I smiled at her but when I turned to leave I could not help but roll my eyes.

I was uncharacteristically nervous about leaving the post office. I peered out the sliding doors to see his truck still sitting in his parking space two spots down. I froze for a second but quickly gained my confidence back as I put on my sunglasses and fixed my hair in the reflection of the glass doors. As I walked to my car, he opened the door to his truck got out, and started to walk over to me. His green eyes were outlined with the thickest eyelashes I had ever seen wasted on a man. He had swagger and was clearly a man's man. In his deep voice, he said "I am sorry again about yesterday when we first met. I don't know where my manners were. My name is Austin Grant. Can I buy you breakfast, or well maybe lunch?" He pulled his cell phone out of his pocket and said "Lunch or even dinner? It is the least I could do." Flipping my long brown hair back and looking at him over my shoulder I respond "Pleased to meet you Austin. My name is Erica Hansen, finally, we know one another's names after all this. Dinner? You're asking me to dinner?" I am completely stunned that he is asking me out. I thought he would think that I was rude after the airport. I couldn't help but be attracted to him. He was gorgeous! "How about you meet me at the Mesa Grill in Sedona or I could pick you up if you like?" Not wanting to reveal where I was staying I responded "I will meet you there at 7 I know exactly where it is." Smiling back at me, tipping the rim of his hat again "See you then."

I watch him drive away as I get into my car. I immediately started to panic because I didn't bring anything that I could wear on a dinner date. What in the hell was I thinking? I did not plan on meeting a sizzling hot cowboy and certainly didn't know what to wear. I decided to keep it simple. I wanted to make an impression but I didn't want to overdress. I decided to wear jeans and a new sweater to dinner. Totally out of character but as they say when in Rome...

Once I got to my hotel room I put some wine in my fridge that I had picked up the day before. I asked room service to send up a wine glass. I ordered a charcuterie tray to tie me over before dinner because I knew I would be too nervous to eat in front of him. I decided to take a long hot bath to try and relax before dinner. In the tub, I couldn't help but think of Austin, his eyes, the smell of his cologne. I remembered talking to that woman at the metaphysical shop. I kept thinking about her and what she told me about the love of my life. Could it be Austin? Nah, I reminded myself I do not believe in that kind of mumbo jumbo.

I got out of the tub and dried myself off feeling very relaxed after my bath. I dried my hair, put on my makeup, and carefully applied my favorite scent to my back, legs, and arms. I slipped into a black bra and new panties that I also purchased on today's shopping spree. I was so nervous and could not decide if I should be fashionably late or be right on time. I wanted to keep him waiting for just a few minutes.

I showed up at Mesa at 7:10 to find him waiting outside. It was chilly out that evening but I could not feel the cold at all. He had on another leather jacket minus the cowboy hat.

For the first time, I was getting a look at his thick mop of brown curly hair. His eyes examined me, scanning my body from head to toe. He took his time looking at me "Erica, you are gorgeous." I smiled "Thank you Austin, should we go inside?" He put his hand on the small of my back and I gasped. I hoped he didn't hear the deep breath I took when I felt his touch. He opened the door for me and the host showed us to a table with a beautiful view of the desert but due to the time of night, there was not much to look at outside. Who needed to look outside when this man sat across the table from me?

He sat down and began our conversation by asking "So Erica, are you new to the area or are you just visiting?" I explained that I was here on vacation. My boss required that I go and completely disconnect from my job. I confessed to him about my work life, "I am a work-a-holic in a male-dominated industry so I guess I try to overcompensate and overachieve but it pays the bills." The conversation is easy. We never seemed to have trouble finding topics of conversation. I told him all about Lisa and Tom. I also confided in him about my failed marriage. He felt that he could confide in me about his life. His mother died when he was 10 so he was raised by his father. Mrs. Perry from the post office has a son who is the same age as Austin. They grew up together and were very close at one time. Her son Jason Perry moved to Colorado, married, and has 2 children now. It seemed like Austin missed his childhood friend but stayed current through his visits with his mother. He admitted to stopping by the post office mainly to visit with her which I thought was incredibly sweet. I thought at that point we had a lot in common. He also lost a parent and knew that heartbreak. His best friend now has a family and moved away from Sedona. I could really identify with him. I also had friends who had moved on and started families. We were both on the same page in life.

He confessed to me that he hadn't had a girlfriend in over a year. I felt he was genuine when he told me that his last relationship fell apart because she didn't want to stay in Sedona. He admitted that she did relocate back to the area after her big dreams seemed to fall apart after moving away for some time. Austin was born and raised in Sedona. He went to college and played football at Arizona State University. He told me he was a business major in college and he had plans to leave the area after college with his girlfriend at the time. His family owned a whole block of buildings that housed many storefronts in Sedona. In Florida we call them strip malls, His dad had passed this off to him to care for after he became sick with cancer. His father was now elderly and lived close to him. His mother passed away when he was 10 years old. Austin felt an overwhelming responsibility to care for his father and the family business. Austin loved Sedona, and clearly had a strong sense of duty to his dad and his legacy.

We enjoyed an amazing dinner, getting lost in conversation while the restaurant was closing around us. I was pleasantly surprised by how easy it was to converse with Austin. I didn't expect him to be so educated. I had clearly put him in the big, dumb, jock cowboy box not realizing he was sensitive, kind, and articulate. We noticed that not many people were left in the restaurant so we decided to leave. He again places his hand on the small of my back as he holds the door open for me. He pulls me in close, wrapping his arms around me. I then begin to feel a brisk gust of wind whip all around us as he pulls me in closer "Erica, I don't want this evening to end." I can barely catch my breath as I stare into his eyes. He takes both hands and touches my face pulling me in for a kiss. I feel his soft full lips press against mine. His beard and mustache were not coarse at all, it was soft and was rich with the smell of his cologne. I felt incredible energy pulsating through every pore, every sense of my being was feeling alive. I didn't want to seem "easy" or promiscuous. "I cannot invite you back to my room Austin I don't even know you." He pulls me in closer and whispers "I feel like I have known you all my life, Erica." My nerves were on edge, I could barely speak. He asked if the hotel had a lounge where we could talk some more. Reluctantly I told him where I was staying and asked if he would like to meet me there for a nightcap.

I get into my car and pull out of the restaurant parking lot followed by Austin this time in a Landrover SUV. I find myself trembling on the way to the hotel. I begin to second guess this decision. Did I just invite a complete stranger back to my hotel? This is not like me at all. I kept thinking that this could be one of the biggest mistakes of my life. Then I started to consider that I was on vacation and so what if I wanted to have a fling? I could leave it all behind when I go back to Tampa and my life. He would not ever run into any of the men I work with so why not? I was trying to weigh the pros and cons but the hotel was a short drive away from the Restaurant and I noticed Austin was right behind me following me closely.

We arrive at the hotel parking lot and Austin quickly finds a parking spot right next to mine. He is at my door opening it for me before I can gather my purse. He helps me out of the car wrapping his arm around me and shielding me from the frigid night air that grew windier. Making our way inside we can't help but notice the temperature difference when stepping inside. There is a fireplace crackling in the lobby. He still keeps his arm wrapped around me as we walk down the hallway. We settled into a cozy place right in front of the fireplace. The conversation flowed, and so did the after-dinner drinks. I began to feel uninhibited, surely it was the alcohol, I am not that free or easy. I am not one who frequently drinks so I am now feeling absolutely no pain. I noticed that he was staring at me while I was chatting away about some nonsense about my job. He smiles and asks "Erica? Are you drunk?" I start to giggle nervously and uncontrollably. He starts to smile and says "Let me make sure you get to your room. I think you have had enough to drink tonight." Laughing still, he grabs my hand and we make our way to my room. He takes my room key and opens the door. "Thank you for a wonderful evening Erica. Are you going to be okay?" I was feeling the room spin at this point and could barely keep myself balanced but did manage to reply, "I will be fine thank you for a great evening." I give him a kiss on the cheek and shut the door.

Once the door was shut the room continued to spin. The last thing I remember was making my way to the bed. I woke up around 4:00 am again with my mouth feeling like it had an old sock for a tongue. I didn't even manage to remove my sweater or bra. My jeans were on the floor. When I managed to get up to get to the bathroom to relieve myself I caught a glimpse of myself in the bathroom mirror. Mascara made me look like a raccoon but I didn't care one bit about that or my morning mouth so I went back to bed until 9:00 am. When I woke I thought it was 9:00 p.m. and not morning. Still dazed from the night before I could not help but think, WOW! I needed coffee. Room service never tasted so good. Coffee and a shower along with some aspirin made me feel somewhat human. I had an intense headache. Thankfully, I knew that I didn't have sex, drunk and incoherent. Clearly, Austin was a gentleman some guys would have taken advantage of a woman wasted out of her mind drunk but he didn't. For a second I wondered if there was something wrong with me.

I was so completely hungover. I kept trying to remember if I made an ass out of myself. I never drink like that. I guess it was the nerves that got the best of me. I was really embarrassed about my behavior. What was I thinking last night? With my sunglasses in tow, I made my way to the lobby where one of the girls who befriended me when I first arrived was smiling with a huge shit-eating grin. I asked, "What are you smiling about?" "Nothing. And Good Morning Erica!" as she giggles and walks away. At that point, she reminded me of Lisa.

When I left the hotel it was a rude awakening, it was a bright, sunny, crisp cool day in Sedona. The sunlight was piercing my hungover eyes. I really didn't want to waste a day of my vacation so I decided to take in some sights. Uptowntown Sedona is rich in history and so picturesque. Everywhere you look it's like you could see this in a postcard. Roundabouts are no joke when one is hungover. I was almost in two collisions before I came across a strip of stores that caught my attention. I parked and found a coffee house and a store that had many souvenirs. I could not control the urge to buy a few more things for Lisa. I purchased a ring that had a polished stone from Sedona that

I loved. Walking down Main Street you get the sense of times gone by. There was no mistaking the southwest vibe. The wild west was still alive in Sedona. The buildings had many nooks and crannies along with beautiful courtyards that had many iron sculptures.

I sat on a bench, sipping my coffee. Out of the corner of my eye, I see a man with a white cowboy hat sweeping the sidewalks. I couldn't tell if it was Austin but I thought it might be. I looked the other way as if I didn't see him at all. Within minutes I hear a voice "Erica? Is that you? How are you feeling today?" He walks over to me with an ear-to-ear grin. "You were feeling no pain last night. Are you okay?" I nodded, squinting, adjusting my sunglasses and scarf "I am just fine thank you, how are you today?" I know my cheeks were red not because of the brisk day but because I was mortified and answered "I am sorry Austin, I guess you could say I am a cheap date. I don't drink very much at all." He laughed "Clearly!" I could not help but feel embarrassed, I could not hold my liquor at all. He certainly didn't seem to mind and I actually think he was amused by it all.

Again, the conversation flowed. He told me that the plaza of stores I was sitting in front of was built and owned by his family for generations. The stores were quaint and were clearly geared for tourism. Just about the time when I felt comfortable again with his presence a woman walks up behind Austin and wraps her arms around his waist. I was taken aback. Who is this blonde bimbo? Why was she this comfortable and brazen and how did she know him? She was petite with short blonde hair and dressed in cowboy boots, skin-tight jeans, and a red sweater. Austin quickly snapped his head around and said "Damn Terry you scared the shit out of me!" Terry was laughing and quipped "You never seemed to mind me grabbing you like this before." Ahhh now the lightbulb goes off in my mind. Is this the old girlfriend? Are they still together? Austin grabbed her hands and put them firmly back at her side saying "That was a long time ago Terry. I would like you to meet a new friend of mine from Florida, Erica, and Erica, this is Terry whom I have known since we were kids." I could feel the contempt vibe as she glared at me. I was annoyed that I was not on my game when meeting his ex-girlfriend or was she really an ex?

Terry was gorgeous. I could see why Austin was attracted to her in the first place. She was clearly a hometown girl. Nothing at all like me, in fact, the complete polar opposite. She had a bob-type haircut with short blonde hair and beautiful blue eyes and seemed to have a very bubbly personality. I could tell she did not care for me at all. Her icy stare indicated that she did not like me talking to Austin. She quickly dismissed my presence and asked "Are you coming to the Festival of Lights this year? I would love to ride the hay ride with you again this year if you are going." Austin looked a little flustered "Not this year Terry and you know why." She smiled "Well if you change your mind I will be there with bells on! Nice to meet you, um what did you say your name was?" Before I could get my name out she flits off.

After she walked away, I could see Austin was not sure how to explain the encounter so I asked, "Was that your ex?" with a nod of his head I knew that he had a major history with this woman. His face was blushed. I noticed he was probably a little embarrassed as it was clear to me he was struggling to find the words. "We ended our romantic relationship permanently last year. I found out she was cheating on me with a buddy of mine after she came back from California. It took a long time for me to get over that kind of betrayal Erica. I am working on it although sometimes it still hurts. We have had an on-again, off-again relationship since we were kids so it wasn't easy."

I couldn't help but be concerned because he looked so flustered after the conversation with the blonde bimbo. I asked him with no regard for his feelings at the time, "Do you still love her?" He took a moment and a deep breath, "I will always love her Erica, We have known each other most of our lives. We tried to make it work but I could not get over the past. I forgave them both but it has been hard to move on. It seems things didn't work out with her and my buddy, but that's not my problem anymore but enough about that. How about lunch?" I knew he was trying anything to avoid the subject so I agreed to a lunch date.

We sat down for an enjoyable lunch and he asked me to come to his house for dinner that evening. I accepted with a lot of reluctance. My mind was racing after meeting his ex. I kept replaying the meeting that just happened on the streets of Sedona over and over in my mind. Was I some fling that he wanted to have to help him get over the bimbo? Why should I even care once I get on that plane to go home there will never be another opportunity to think about this again. Afterall, I had a life and a career in Florida and Austin was committed to Sedona.

I went back to the hotel to take a nap before getting ready to go to his house. After a peaceful rest, I showered, put on another pair of jeans, and made my way to the hotel lobby. One of the girls smiled and asked, "Going out again Erica?" "Why yes, yes I am going out again." With another toothy grin, she responded "Have a great time!"

Once in my car, I plugged his address into the GPS. It's almost dark now at 6 p.m. which is a cause for concern while driving in Sedona. I thought about making him pick me up but I wanted to be sure to have a way out if I wanted to leave. I started to consider that I was going to a strange man's home that I just met. What if he was some kind of serial killer? I shrugged off that notion. There was no way this sweet guy could be a killer.

My GPS took me up a steep road called Smoke Trail Lane. Once I had reached the destination I noticed big iron gates with a giant "G" on the doors. I pulled up to the call box and dialed the main house, upon the opening of the gates the house was amazing. There was a gazebo and courtyard area. Huge double teak wood doors graced the entry where Austin was waiting. He was wearing jeans of course with his signature flannel shirt, this time red and black buffalo checked which had always been my favorite. He dashed over to my door and opened it while helping me out of the car. "Welcome to my home Erica." The house seemed to blend into the landscape. It was terracotta color, with a real adobe type theme. Once entering through the big teak doors your eye goes to the 24-foot high ceilings with skylights. A majestic fireplace with floor-to-ceiling windows that open up to the terrace.

The outside terrace had a rustic outdoor kitchen that overlooked a stunning pool and heated spa. This area had a waterfall, decorative boulders, and natural granite that local artists hand-built for the Grant family. The fire pit had a roaring fire that took the chill out of the air when pulling up a chair close to it. I glanced to see a woman who seemed to be cooking dinner inside. I asked Austin "Who is that inside?" "That is our housekeeper Velma. Actually, she is more than a housekeeper. She helped raise me after my mother passed away. She has been a great help to my father over the years."

I could tell Velma was Native American. She had long salt and pepper hair tied back into a tight bun, a dark complexion, and eyes. Short and stocky wearing a purple sweat suit while cooking something that smelled amazing. She sees me through the big picture window and waves with a smile that could light up the whole patio. She walks out with a plate of empanada appetizers "Welcome Miss Erica, would you like to try some homemade salsa with your empanadas? Mr. Austin has been so excited that you are coming here tonight." As I glance at Austin I can see he is looking back at Velma with a frown while mouthing "stop". I knew she would be a source of great information at this point and I could not wait to pick her brain. She sets the plate down on a table and waves with a giggle, cute little smile, and wink to scurry off to continue her work in the kitchen.

"You invited me to dinner. I thought it would be you cooking." He smirked "You do want to eat don't you?" "So, you don't cook?" "I only grill Erica." I immediately thought to myself, is that a guy thing? Why is it that most men I know only grill? I didn't care if he knew how to cook or not. His handsome face highlighted by the warm glow of the fire was mesmerizing. I was feeling spellbound by this man. It was not like me to be so enchanted. I felt something in the pit of my stomach that I never felt before when looking at him as he was smiling back at me. Could I actually be falling for this cowboy? I then heard the patio doors open and Velma loudly "Get back here!" Looking back at the house I see a yellow flash. I knew that the devil dog was on the loose again. I am standing by the pool as I watch Winston bolting right for me. I brace myself for impact. As I hear Austin saying "Winston, NO!" This beast jumps on me, making me lose my balance. I start to stumble backward, panic must have washed over my face as Winston and I plunged right into the pool!

As I come up for air I see Austin laughing, uncontrollably while Winston swims to the steps and jets over to Austin. The water is warm due to what I assume is solar but I knew the minute I got out it would be a shock with the frigid night air. Velma already had 2 big fluffy towels in her hands as she started to apologize. "Miss Erica I am so sorry he is so fast. Let me get a robe for you and put your clothes in the dryer." Now I am angry, the icy night air after getting out of the pool did not impact the heat that was generated from my body. I was so pissed this dog knocked me right into a pool. I thanked Velma, "That won't be necessary, I am leaving." Austin still could not keep a straight face which enraged me even more. "You would do well to send that dog to obedience school Austin, he is a menace." The statement made him laugh harder still. "Have a nice life!" I grabbed my purse and my coat and started heading for the front doors dripping all the way.

"Please wait, I am sorry and yes you are right he does need to go to puppy school." I am continuing my path straight to the rental car, dripping all the way through his magnificent foyer. Austin is following behind me, "Erica, please wait!" I get out the door and make my way to the car. I open my car door and start the engine. As I rolled down my window on my way down the driveway I then once again extended my middle finger as I left. I could still see him laughing in my rearview mirror as I rolled down the driveway which infuriated me even more.

I arrived at the hotel, still dripping wet walking into the lobby. My two girls stopped dead in their tracks as they watched me drip past them. I put my hand up and said I raise my hand and say "Don't say a single word ladies!" as I hurried past them. Once in my room, I took a hot shower. My phone was going off. It was Austin, texting me an apology. I didn't care, as I slipped into my comfortable PJs and snuggled into my comfy bed while silencing my ringer on my phone.

I slept in till around 8:30 and that is sleeping in by my standards. I ordered room service, my usual coffee, and fresh fruit. I hear a knock at the door, thinking it was room service. I open the door to see a huge bouquet of red roses. The bellman said "Flower delivery for you miss. Where would you like me to put them?" I knew immediately they were from Austin. I snatched the card away from him to open the card. It read "Let's kiss and make up, Austin" I turned to the bellman "These flowers would look perfect in your lobby. I suggest you take them there because I do not want them." He replies "Yes ma'am!"

I left the hotel to find another gloriously brisk day in Sedona. I decided to go to the same mall to see if I could find something else for Lisa. The sun was out, the wind was whipping which isn't what I am used to at all. I was beginning to miss the warmth and humidity of the Tampa Bay area, but I was going to make the best of it. I decided to go to the same metaphysical shop that I had visited the other day. I did eye a beautiful pendant that I knew Lisa would love.

Once I got through several roundabouts I found the shop again. I parked and walked in to smell an aroma of incense that was unfamiliar but very pleasant. I struck up a conversation with a woman who claimed to be a reader. She was middle-aged, with long dark straight hair. She was wearing a long black dress and she had on a shawl that was weaved with a very unique-looking material. I asked her if she made it and she told me it was a gift. She smiled and asked, "Are you looking for answers to your questions today?" I smiled and admitted that I had never experienced this type of thing before and it made me a little uncomfortable. "I have had a spiritual reading." The woman replied, "Isn't it about time?"

I decided to throw caution to the wind and try something new. After all, I wasn't getting all my hair cut off or getting a tattoo. This was something I could take with a grain of salt and do for fun. I asked her if she had the time to give me a reading and she quickly responded "Why yes I do. You were led here by your spirit guides and I am obligated to give you a reading. I would not want to disappoint your guide from the other side." I couldn't help but wonder who and what this woman was talking about.

We made our way upstairs to a room that was dimly lit. Everywhere I looked there were things that promoted peaceful thoughts. I noticed affirmations on the walls of positivity. There was a small table with two chairs. The table had a deep purple colored felt type table cloth. There were 3 decks of cards on the table with a large crystal ball. She had a variety of other crystals on the table. I also noticed an abalone shell with some kind of dried herb inside it with a feather on top of it. I asked her what that might be for. She told me it was to release the room of any negative energy. With that, she lit the herb inside which had a pungent smell to it that I did not like at all. I asked her "What is that stuff, it smells nasty!" She got a kick out of my response. "It takes some getting used to the smell, but you have a lot of negativity surrounding your aura that I need to cleanse to get a good reading on you."

I sat down and watched her while she moved around the room asking to bless me, the room, and her cards. She also asked for the blessing to guide me in my journey and to give thanks in advance for the opportunity to meet me and help me along my way. Once she sat down in front of me she asked "What are your name and birthdate?" When I told her she introduced herself to me. "My name is Jaya, I am happy to give you your very first spiritual reading" I was totally intrigued, she went on "You have come to Sedona to find yourself?" I told her that I wanted to experience a vortex. I told her that I was a busy business professional with no time for self-reflection or self-care. She advised me that this would be unlike anything I had ever experienced before. She asked me to clear my thoughts and take some deep breaths in, then hold it for a few seconds and exhale deeply three times.

I began to relax slightly although my thoughts raced as I tried to breathe as she instructed. I noticed that she lit a large white candle that was on the table. She picked up a deck of cards that had beautiful angels on it. Each card had some kind of message on it. She asked me to shuffle the deck and concentrate on what led me here to Sedona. I shuffled the deck and a card dropped out of my hands. She stopped me and said, "That's a message!" She picked up the card to find a beautiful angel holding a staff. The angel was female with long dark brown hair and on the card, it said simply "Believe in yourself." She then asked me to lay the cards down on the table and pick another. I picked another card and turned it over to see another angel, this one was obviously male. The card was beautiful and read "You're on a path of Joy!"

Jaya was pleased by what I had picked for the cards. I didn't really see the significance. She went on to pick up yet another deck of cards. She began to shuffle the deck with her eyes closed. She looked like she was in a trance. She placed the cards in three stacks. She asked me to pick a stack. I selected the biggest stack in the middle, and she then picked up the rest of the cards and started to place them in some kind of formation. She began to explain to me the meaning of the cards and the meaning of the placement. "I see that you have come from far away. A tropical climate?" "Why yes, Florida as a matter of fact." "I see that you are in charge of a lot of things. A lot of men, who think you are not knowledgeable?" I laugh "Right again!" She takes a moment to look at another card and draws one from the pile and places it on top of another card. Jaya smiled "You found true love here. You have your doubts but it's a real love. You will need to open your heart to it or it may pass you by."

I am puzzled at this point. "What do you mean pass me by?" She explained, "Things can change. Nothing is set in stone and the universe will respond when you reject whatever gift it is trying to give you. If you are not receptive it will not give you the blessing." She was pulling cards from the pile and then said "You will be disappointed by your new love. You should not be too critical. You must give it a chance because you will find it very gratifying. I see that you will be moving to be with this man. It looks like you will be moving here to Sedona." I begin to laugh "I have a job, a well-paying job in Florida, and a life!" She quickly responded "You have a JOB in Florida. You have no life. I see you sitting eating ice cream and pumpkin pie on your couch in your pajamas. That is NOT a life my dear." I nod back at her in shame. How could she possibly know about that? "You're right about that, but my job is my life and earns me a great living." With a deep inhale, she responds "You are not living. You are only existing. You will leave Florida, you will come here and may have some trouble finding what you want to do professionally here in Arizona but you will not have to work, you will be useful to your partner." I scoffed "You don't know me very well" She said "No, I don't but your guides and angels do and that's where I am getting my information from. You will have challenges as many couples do starting out but you will be blissfully happy with him if you would only give it a chance."

She gave me some advice on how to properly meditate. I told her that I had problems clearing my mind and that I never thought I could do it effectively. She told me to concentrate on my breathing only and to try to focus on that. She advised me to go back to the airport where I met Austin and try again. She said it is one of the most powerful vortex locations in Sedona. I didn't want to tell her about meeting Austin there. I wanted to see if she was the real deal or if she was some kind of gypsy ready to fleece people for money.

She did tell me things that had happened in my life. She told me that I was an only child and that I was married once before with no children. I was shocked when she told me that I lost my parents in a car crash and they were with me at all times. I became emotional when she described my parents to me in great detail. She told me that my mother was an educated woman who was also a real estate broker. My father was a mortgage broker. They made the perfect couple. They were so professional and gave back to the community. At the time of their death, I found out that they had left a large life insurance policy naming me as the beneficiary. Money had never been an issue for me in my adult life since they passed because they loved me enough to care for me after their deaths. I almost found myself becoming emotional when she passed on a message that they still watch over me. How could she possibly know that too?

I left the room feeling as though I somehow evolved. I thanked Jaya for her reading. She told me that I could call her from Florida if I ever needed to talk. I left the shop and barely got into my car before I felt tears streaming down my face. I could sense that she was right about my parents. I knew they were always with me but the validation was profound.

I knew I had to go back to the airport. I drove to the area where I had met Austin and the devil dog. I noticed three cars at the site where I had parked before. I decided to wait there a few minutes to compose myself. I asked the universe for guidance just like Jaya told me to do. After some time had passed a few people came down the pathway and got into the cars that were parked next to me. I immediately bolted from my car and made my way up the winding path to the clearing. There was a large red boulder that looked over the canyon. I sat on top of it with my legs crossed. I gazed upon the canyon below. It was majestic and breathtakingly beautiful. There were prickly pear cacti everywhere. Large white oak trees and juniper plants peppered the landscape. I took a deep breath in while taking in the beauty that was right before me. I whispered "Thank you for this moment in time. I ask for guidance so I may feel my first vortex. Please send my angels and spirit guides to this location to assist me! Please!"

I began to breathe just like Jaya instructed me to do. I closed my eyes and began to focus only on my breathing. I started to sense a vibration that seemed like it was coming right from the boulder that I was sitting on. The nape of my neck and shoulders had a palpable sensation. It felt like all the hair on my arms and neck, even my hair felt electrified. My skin was tingling as I continued to breathe and focused only on the sensations and my breath. I felt as if I were free for the first time in my life! I felt that I was recharged and inspired. I felt alive!

I didn't realize that one hour had passed as I sat on that rock. I began to hear people making their way up the pathway so I got off the rock that I was sitting on. Before I got down I thanked my guides and angels for their assistance per Jaya's advice. Feeling so grateful for the experience I made my way back to my rental car. I had left my phone inside so that I would not be disturbed while attempting to feel a vortex. I noticed that Austin had called 4 times. He left only one message on the last call saying "Erica, please call me back. I would love to see you and try to make it up to you, but I won't bother you or call you again. The ball is in your court."

I kept thinking about my reading. Was I about to give up on the best thing that could possibly happen to me? I had asked for guidance as I meditated on top of that boulder. I kept getting the feeling that I should give Austin a chance. After all, let's face facts, he was the first man in years that even piqued my interest. I reluctantly picked up my phone and returned his call. He sounded genuinely relieved to hear from me. He told me that his housekeeper Velma was very upset about what happened and felt responsible for letting Winston escape. She wanted me to come back to sample her cooking so she could make amends. I reluctantly agreed to return that evening for dinner at 6 with an understanding that we would not be sitting outside anywhere near the pool.

I arrived at 6:15 to find Austin and Velma at the front door awaiting my arrival. This time they have Winston on a leash. They are all happy to see me, especially Winston. His tail was wagging and I swear to you he was smiling. Velma apologized profusely. "Miss Erica, it's all my fault. Winston is getting too strong for me. I didn't mean for him to knock you over. Please accept my apology. Mr. Austin has been so upset since this happened." I smiled "Velma, it's okay. Let's not talk about it again. It's over with."

We walk into an adobe-style, modern dwelling that is so perfect for the area. The living area had wood beams stretching across the whole span of the ceiling that towered

25 feet with a stone fireplace crackling in the far corner. Austin grabbed my hand and led me to the couch group in front of the fireplace, "I think this would be more comfortable for us to sit and get to know each other better don't you think?" I nodded and sat down.

Velma brings in a charcuterie board loaded with cheeses, meats, and marinated vegetables. She also makes herself scarce. After dropping off the food she and Winston go out the double doors to the pool deck area. When I asked, "Where are they going?" Austin replies "They are going to Velma's to keep him out of trouble tonight."

Velma is a fantastic cook. She outdid herself with an authentic meal indigenous to the region. She did not seem to want to stick around at all and retreated to the kitchen area. After we finished the second bottle of wine, I began to loosen up a bit. As usual, the conversation was easy. As we looked into each other's eyes he leaned in for a long deep kiss. I couldn't remember ever feeling this way about anyone ever before. That feeling in the pit of my stomach was back. I could not get enough of his soft lips. His strong hands caressed my shoulders and back. He whispered, "Would you like to go to my room?" I responded without hesitation "Yes. Why yes Austin I would."

He stands up and scoops me up as if I were weightless. I grab him around his neck as I begin to wonder again if I am making a mistake. That thought quickly passed as he started kissing my neck as he made his way down the hallway to a dimly lit area that I quickly figured out was his bedroom. It also had a large fireplace that was lit with warmth emanating from the hearth. The large four-poster bed was so comfortable with pillows scattered across the comforter. As he lay me down his lips continued to kiss my neck. He started to unbutton my shirt exposing my breast bone which he gently kissed as he was feeling my breasts. My hands were in his curly brown hair. I could not get enough of him. I felt his body pressing against mine, I could feel his heart beating in his chest and his bulge growing larger the longer we kissed. We started to undress each other while kissing every part that was exposed. I know things are moving quickly but I don't care at all.

Austin took lovemaking to a whole new level. I had no idea that I could ever feel so adored, worshiped, and loved by a man. He was gentle and forceful at the same time. Making sure to give me pleasure before satisfying himself all while completely taking his time. It's as if time were standing still while we were embracing each other's souls.

As I lay there totally vulnerable to him I began to hear footsteps coming down the hallway. They sounded like a woman's high heels! With no warning, the lights come on in the bedroom. At the door stands Terry, his ex-girlfriend! She is dressed in a fur coat, boots, a black bra, and black panties to match with nothing else on at all! As she stands at the doorway she exclaims, "Well isn't this awkward?"

Austin shouts "What the hell are you doing here?" I am in total shock at this point. I feel so embarrassed about the whole situation. I begin to grab my clothes from the floor while trying to button up my shirt and pants. Austin is already at the doorway having a shouting match with Terry as I am trying to get out of there with some shred of dignity. He is obviously upset about this situation but I can't help but wonder why she still has a key or how she is able to get access to his place. It's all his fault!

Again I find myself in a completely compromising situation and for the second time now at this man's house! What was I thinking! I start to get my things together as I try to get past Terry and Austin at the bedroom doorway, I am frantically looking for my purse and boots as I hear Austin yelling "You cheated on ME! So there is nothing left between us! You need to go on with your life and let me go on with mine!" As I hear Terry respond "Let you go on with life and that slut you just met?" Now, that stopped me in my tracks. I turned and said quietly and calmly "You have a lot of nerve calling me a slut as you stand in your ex-boyfriend's doorway looking like a stripper. Where's your pole?" Austin roars with laughter but that quickly subsides as he sees me dressed, coat on, and heading for the front door. "Erica, please don't go! Somebody else needs to go!" He turns back to look at Terry "You're not welcome here anymore, get out!"

I had to keep focused on the pathway to the front door and to get into my car. I have never been so freaked out by a situation before. My flight leaves in 3 days but I could not stand the thought of staying in Sedona another day. I didn't want to run into Austin again or even worse Terry! I made arrangements to change my flight to leave at 11:00 a.m. the next morning. I was determined to leave Sedona in the dead of night. I did not want to give Austin the opportunity to send flowers or come to my hotel.

I noticed that I had three missed calls from Austin. He didn't leave any messages. I also notice a text from him simply saying "Please let's talk." I didn't answer the text or return the calls. I just wanted to go back to the warmth of Tampa. I didn't want to even think about Sedona again. I called for the bellhop to help with my luggage as I loaded up to go home. The drive to Phoenix had me reliving my experiences with Austin. I replayed the night before over and over in my head. On the plane, I kept thinking about Austin and wondering if my rash behavior may have killed my one chance for true love. Then I started to think about Terry. Could I live with that interference for the rest of our lives? Was he really over her? I began to realize I didn't live in Sedona. Long-distance relationships never work out. I had a life and responsibilities at home and it was time to put this nightmare vacation behind me.

When landing in Tampa, the captain announced it was 80 degrees when we started our approach. The sun was shining and I could see the bay waters glistening from the window of the plane. I was so overjoyed to be home, I missed the warm sun and even missed the humidity in the air. I really didn't want to call Lisa and let her know that I had left early. I planned to take refuge in my condo and indulge in ice cream and takeout while staying in my pajamas and eating a small truckload of ice cream for the next three days of my vacation. This is what I was used to.

When Monday came I was eager to start my work week. Oddly enough, I really missed the chaos of my job and of course Lisa. I didn't even want to explain what happened to me in Sedona. As I was leaving for the office I could not help but notice the difference in temperatures from Sedona, being grateful for the sun on my face with the warmth of the gentle sea breeze that I missed so much. Lisa was waiting for me in my office. "WELL? Tell me what happened? Did you enjoy yourself?" I couldn't help but roll my eyes "Lisa, I really don't want to discuss the miserable time I had in

Sedona. I just want to get caught up on what happened here when I was away." Looking so defeated "Really Erica? You didn't have any fun at all? I am sorry I feel responsible for sending you there." I quickly answered her back "Not your fault. I am a grown woman. Don't you worry about my disastrous vacation. Not your problem."

Lisa sat in front of my desk in her usual chair. "Erica, I know something happened while you were away. If you are not going to talk to me about it, who will you discuss this with?" I began to break down and cry. Lisa looked shocked. It is so out of character for me to sob at my desk. "Erica you are not alright!" I began to tell her all about Austin. It felt good to vent to somebody about what happened. Bouncing it off of somebody who is level-headed like Lisa was just what I needed. She thought I may have been too quick to judge the events that led me to an early flight. She thought I should have given Austin an opportunity to explain. I told Lisa that was not going to happen. I thought it was just a fling and it is now over and I needed to just move on.

I did have a goodie bag for Lisa, things that I found in Sedona that I thought she might like. I watched her eyes light up as she opened up her bag filled with some jewelry that was indigenous to the region. I also found a dream catcher and some stones and rocks from the shop where I had my reading. I brushed it all off because I didn't want to get into the details again with Lisa and relive my tragic story. I knew that she had her hands full with me on vacation. I took a deep breath in and said "Let's just get to work."

The day was long, and even though I had three solid days of eating ice cream and binge-watching Netflix I still felt emotionally exhausted. I cried myself to sleep every night since I returned home. If this is what love feels like you can have it. After a longer-than-usual Monday, I couldn't wait to get back to my condo and hide away. Austin had called many times since I left Sedona. I would not respond to his calls or texts. I was really ready to close that door. I never wanted to see him or go out west again.

I left for the day and started to feel a little guilty about hiding away. It was such a gorgeous day in Tampa I decided to get out instead of burying my head in the sand and walking in an area that I absolutely love. The Tampa Riverwalk is a pedestrian trail that follows the Hillsborough River. I was watching the river taxis float by as I sat on a bench near the Curtis Hixon waterfront park area. Trying to forget about Austin was more difficult than I imagined. The sun was beginning to set and there was a pink and orange hue to the sky that reflected off the water in the river. I was in a trance-like state thinking about how Austin made me feel. I remembered his strong, muscular arms and how I felt so safe with him holding me tightly.

The sun was almost set and I looked down the riverwalk to see a man walking towards me. He had on a baseball cap with jeans and a gray sweatshirt. I sensed that I knew this person, I actually thought it may have been one of the contractors that I worked with. Once I got closer I realized it wasn't a contractor, it was Austin! I wanted to duck and walk away but I was so shocked by his presence and asked "What are you doing here? How did you find me?" He said "I called your workplace and spoke to a person who I know cares about you not only as an employer but as a true friend. I really like your assistant, Lisa, she told me about you

Erica. She knows you like a book and did clue me on where to find you. Please don't be mad at her but I remembered where you worked and I called your office. I decided to come to Tampa to try to find you. I could not let things end the way they did with us. I got in last night and I am staying right there at the Hilton. I decided to go for a walk to watch the sunset and here you are! It's like I was meant to find you, Erica! Please, let's talk. I have come so far to find you."Nobody had ever traveled thousands of miles to see me. He didn't know if I would slam the door in his face even if he did find me. I was totally disarmed.

We sat on the bench and talked about the disastrous dinner date. "I think your house is jinxed because every time I am there something terrible happens." He told me that he had no intentions of ever getting back with Terry. The betrayal he felt when she cheated on him with his friend was still painful but he felt he learned from that experience and would not go back to Terry. I could tell that he was still hurt by the look in his eyes. His green eyes were truly the windows to his soul. He was a tender-hearted person, it was totally obvious to me. He kissed my hand and looked into my eyes "Please forgive me, Erica, I can't stand it when you are mad at me. Can we just start over in your town? I have a few days before I need to get back home. Will you show me around?" I sighed "I'd love to!"

He gave me a long deep kiss as we sat on the bench watching the boats float by. We started to walk down the trail and found ourselves in front of his hotel. "Well, it seems as if you have walked me to *my* door." "Why yes, looks like I got you back to your room safely." We both giggle. He wraps his arm around my shoulder as we make our way up to his hotel room. I can't believe this is happening. How is he here? I tried not to read too much into the situation and for once in my miserable uptight life, I decided to live and love freely.

We cannot keep our hands off of each other as we get off the elevator. When he gets the key inside the automatic lock we almost stumble into his room as we are undressing one another in a frenzy. I never had a man hold me this way or be so attentive. When falling asleep in his arms I could not feel more safe, secure, and dare I say loved.

I woke up around 4 a.m. to see him sound asleep. His toned butt was exposed and I could not help but caress it, waking him from a sound sleep. "Where are you going?" with a bit of a growl "Work, oh how I hate to leave. I can get out early today, so I will text you right after lunch?" He pulls me in for a deep kiss that makes me want to forget about the workday and stay in bed with Austin. I do come back to my senses and realize that Monty would require my work to be completed on a large project so I had no choice but to go into the office.

I put in a short day after Lisa and I talked a little bit about Austin. She was thrilled that I had found somebody who I actually had feelings for but even more excited to know that he followed me back to Tampa and I was happy that he did. I was a little upset about her giving him information but that is Lisa. She is one to take a chance on love. She talked to Austin several times when I was hibernating when I came home early from Sedona. Lisa already knew all about my trip before I even made it into the office, well she knew about Austin. She was thrilled when I told her I would be taking the next couple of days off to show Austin my city. I had called Monty to let him know that I would need a couple of days to recover from my vacation and I got his blessing.

I texted Austin to be ready and I would pick him up to show him around. The next three days we had such a wonderful time. We went to lunch at the Columbian Restaurant. We had a great time walking through Ybor City. Austin was amazed by the wild chickens that were running loose there. He was stunned by the beauty of Tampa although he had traveled here when he was playing college football. When he was here he didn't have enough time to take in any sites when he was in college. We went to several beaches even though the weather was a little brisk. In December you can have a variety of different temperatures in Florida. You just need to be prepared for any weather conditions. We did a boat tour down the Hillsborough River, and we went north to Weeki Wachee Springs to kayak and see manatees. We had fun-filled days seeing the sights and passion-filled evenings in my condo for a romantic few days.

When it came time for Austin to return to Sedona it was more devastating than I had anticipated. I went to his hotel room so I could take him to the airport. He opened the door and invited me in. He sat down at the end of the bed and grabbed my hands while looking up at me. He pulled me in closer as I grabbed a tuft of his brown curly hair and I pulled his hair slightly to lean his head back, I leaned down for a long deep kiss. He whispered in my ear, "Erica, I am crazy about you. I can't imagine life without you in it now that I have found you I don't ever want to let you go." We cannot keep our hands off of each other. As he pulled me down to the bed I whispered, "You're going to miss your flight." He only sighs as he continues to undress and leave me breathless.

We stumbled out of bed while both of us checked our phones for the time. He looked frantic and asked, "How long does it take to get to the airport?" I kissed him on the cheek and said "I got this, let's go I will get you there in time." We rolled up to the drop-off zone at the airport where the airport police get very aggressive if you stay too long. He kissed me again the way only Austin could. I began to feel tears, was I actually crying? I was crying! I never wanted a man to have that kind of power over me. I tried to gain composure but when I looked at Austin's green eyes he also had tears in his eyes. "I don't want to leave you, Erica, I am going to miss you so much. Can you come again for a visit soon?" I knew that he had responsibilities to care for his aging father and the building he managed. "I am not sure when I can come out again. I will let you know. We will talk soon, no set rules. We will see one another soon!" He nods while kissing both of my hands. "You better get to the terminal."

After he leaves I am overwhelmed with loneliness. I feel that my reading with Jaya was spot on, I did meet the love of my life in Sedona. I was now watching him fly home and I would be alone again for Christmas. Was this what I really wanted? To spend another holiday alone in my condo eating takeout?

I went to the office the next day after crying myself to sleep the night before. I really did miss Austin. I was afraid that it was only due to the holiday but I did miss him. I missed his smile, his scent, and most of all his kisses. When I got in Lisa was waiting to hear all about the romantic times that I had in the last couple of days. I started to feel a little sad once again and didn't want to show that emotion in my office setting. Lisa looked up from her laptop and said "Erica, you're human! If you want to be with him for Christmas just GO!" I don't know if I was just seeking out somebody's permission but as soon as she said to go, I made up my mind that I was going.

Lisa had booked a flight that cost a small fortune. I didn't care one bit. I knew I had to be with him for Christmas. I had to transfer twice before reaching Flagstaff airport. This airport was very close to the Grand Canyon which I wanted to see on the last trip but I left early due to the drama that happened. Not caring at all about the Canyon I left for Sedona carefully calculating a route that would not take me through the mountains.

I reached Sedona at around 6:00 p.m. and had full intention of driving right to Austin's house to surprise him. When I arrived at the gate I found them wide open which I thought to be very odd. I pulled up to his house to hear very loud music playing. It seems as if I interrupted a party. Apparently, Austin was not sitting at home lonely the way I was. He was throwing a damn shindig! I got out of my car and made my way inside to see Velma hard at work in the kitchen. She didn't even notice that I was there. I walked out to the pool patio area where I observed Austin dancing with Terry. It wasn't just dancing. They moved like they were in tune with one another's body and the group of friends were cheering them on. I had no idea that Austin being his size could salsa dance like that. They were putting on a show and it was like it had been rehearsed. Terry was totally into it and I know she saw me out of the corner of her eye. About that time she grabbed Austin and pulled him in for a kiss. I was stunned at the sight of them embarrassed while Terry kissed him. I left that house again sobbing. I almost knocked Velma over as I ran through the front door. She yelled out "Miss Erica where are you going?"

I got into my car and drove it like the devil himself was chasing me down. I didn't care where I was going, I just wanted to get out of Sedona. I ended up driving straight back to Flagstaff. I decided to get a hotel room there. I couldn't be selective because it was 4 days before Christmas Eve. I called Lisa to ask her to help me book a flight home as soon as humanly possible no matter what the cost. She was concerned but I couldn't explain at the time it was too painful to even discuss with Lisa. Seeing Austin and Terry together that way made me wonder why he would want me at all. They seemed to fit together perfectly. He looked so happy when he was dancing with her. I could not get that image out of my mind.

Lisa was able to book a flight out the next evening at 7:30 p.m. which would have put me in Tampa at 4:00 a.m. after two flight changes but I didn't care. I decided to go to the Grand Canyon to look around before my flight. I know it to be one of the wonders of the world and the North Rim is rumored to have vortex locations. I made my way to the welcome center. I came to the canyon rim and I really could not believe my eyes. What a mind-blowing experience! I sat on a bench at the rim and sobbed. I thought I made a total ass out of myself by chasing this cowboy back here to Arizona when he is clearly not over his ex. The wind whistles around me with an eerie sound. I was too emotional to feel anything but cold and sad so I got to my rental car and made my way to the airport. I reflected on the reading I had in Sedona with Jaya. I kept thinking that she was wrong, wrong about Austin. Wrong about true love, and wrong about me relocating to Sedona!

I arrived in Tampa on the redeye and could not wait to get to my condo. The next day I had planned to just relax and stay inside. I didn't want to go out at all and prepared to hibernate once again. I was back to being my introverted self, licking my wounds in a quart of ice cream. Austin was calling every couple of hours. He left two voice messages that I chose to ignore. His text messages were short and sweet just asking to talk. I chose to ignore them as well.

Christmas Eve was an evening I detested. Since I had no family that time of year was difficult enough, but when you throw in the heartbreak I was feeling for Austin on top of that it made that evening totally miserable! Around 4:00 p.m. I decided to watch Netflix and make a frozen pizza. I couldn't help but ask…My life has come to this?

I popped the pizza in the oven and heard a knock at my door. I had no clue who was there and didn't care. I wasn't going to answer. Then the knock happened again, I still didn't answer. The third knock was a little louder but not evasive so I got up to look through the peephole and could not see a thing! Through the door, I asked, "Who is it?" "Delivery Ma'am"

I opened the door to find Austin standing there with his white cowboy hat holding 2 dozen red long-stem roses. "Merry Christmas Erica!" I tried to slam the door on him but he wedged it with his cowboy boot. "Please let me in so we can talk. I came a long way once again to see you. Please don't turn me away and let me explain." I respond sharply, "You are clearly not over her, you are in denial if you think you are. I am not willing to be hurt by you or anybody else for that matter. I think you should leave. What are we doing anyway? You live there, I live here, what's the point?" "The point is Erica, I am in love with you. I have never felt so happy in all my life. I have never felt this way for a woman. I can't imagine my life without you." I gulped and must have looked like a deer caught in the headlights of a speeding car. "You don't really mean that, how do you expect me to believe that?" He grabbed both of my hands while his green eyes focused on me "I love you Erica, and I don't want to live without you in my life."

I was flushed and felt blindsided. Here I was standing in my doorway with my PJs on, and no make-up, and I knew my hair was wild but here I was looking at this gorgeous man telling me how much he adores me. Am I dreaming again?

I invited him to come inside where we sat on my couch as he explained the events that led up to me seeing him with Terry. Every year his family puts on a Christmas party for those vendors who rent stores from him. It's like a company Christmas party. Terry has a store in the building. She sells soaps, souvenirs, and miscellaneous items. Terry's mother was at the party and asked them to dance a routine they had done for a contest where they actually won first prize. Terry was "caught up in the moment" according to Austin. "When she kissed me like that I was totally surprised. I wasn't expecting that. I knew something was up when Velma told me you were at my house and it blew me away that you came back to Sedona. I knew Terry did that on purpose because she saw you there! She was trying to make you jealous. Apparently, it worked. I don't care about her. I care about you, Erica. Only you! Please tell me you feel the same way. Or was I just a fling that you wanted to have when you were on vacation? I hope you feel the same way about me as I do you."

I am reluctant to reveal my true feelings especially with a man but with Austin, I felt differently. "I do care for you Austin, I feel like I am falling in love with you too. I just don't know where this could possibly go. You have commitments in Sedona as I do here. I have a career and a life here." I couldn't help but bring up my past relationship. "My ex-husband is with a much younger woman right now and expecting their first child. Having a family is what broke up our marriage. He wanted a child more specifically a son, and I didn't want one at that time. How do you feel about kids? It can be a deal breaker for couples who feel differently." He sat back and had a deep thoughtful look on his handsome face. "Erica, I have never thought about having children. The very thought terrifies me. If I were to consider having a family it would have to be a mutual decision between us. I would never pressure you to have a child because it would be you to carry and deliver a baby." It seemed that he had all the right answers. Then I started to contemplate my life here in Florida. It's Christmas Eve and I am having frozen pizza alone. Is that leading a life that is fulfilling and satisfying? As I stared into his green eyes I knew that he was my future, my cowboy, my gentleman. I knew if I were to drop dead Monty would fill my position. My ego thought it would take him weeks if not months to fill my position but realistically, I knew within a matter of days he would have my seat filled.

We spent Christmas together in my condo. We ate frozen pizza and had ice cream in bed. We did watch some movies but most of the time we spent those few days was in my bedroom. We talked so much about the future. We made plans to go back to Sedona together. We both knew a long-distance relationship would not work out. I knew he could not leave his father or his family's business. I also knew it was a total leap of faith but I decided to lease out my condo and I advised Monty that I would be relocating to Sedona. Monty asked if I would return to do some consulting work on occasion which I happily agreed to. I recommended that he promote Lisa to a position that would elevate her financially. She was so organized and deserving of more than just an admin assistant position. Monty assured me he would take good care of her.

Austin and I planned to go back to Sedona together. As a team and faced whatever life was going to throw at us as a unit. At first, I hated the thought of quitting my job, and moving terrified me. I had savings from the life insurance that my parents left me so I felt comfortable financially making this kind of change. I planned on taking the year off to get to know Austin before I would look for work in Arizona. Austin and I had decided that I would move in with him after he changed all the locks and gate codes so we would not have any more surprise visits. I was going to be out of my comfort zone but Austin's house was big enough and had enough outdoor living space to make things very cozy for us.

I started the process of moving across the county. At first, it was totally overwhelming, but as the weeks went by, and the more I came back to Florida to pack up and tie up all loose ends the easier it was to adjust to the idea of moving to Sedona full time. I did not plan to take much with me other than clothes. My condo would be leased with all my furniture so really it was not as bad as I had imagined. I was even getting used to the driving conditions on the roads in the mountains whenever I returned to Arizona.

In the weeks that followed I got to know Austin's father Phillip. His father had physical challenges but his mind was as sharp as a tack. We had many conversations mainly about Austin when he was a boy. Austin didn't like his dad telling all his dirty childhood secrets. I found them to be thoroughly charming and entertaining. Phillip didn't care for Terry at all. We had that in common. He didn't like that she broke Austin's heart and thought she was a "golddigger." I started to visit him twice a week and bring him lunch to offer his caregiver some time off. I genuinely enjoyed talking to Phillip, he was a real-life pioneer of the area in every sense of the word and a true father figure that I had missed since my parents died. He was strong and kind. He talked about Austin's mother Rosalee all the time. He paid me the ultimate compliment and said I reminded him of her when she was young. He would mention every day how much he loved and missed her. I could see the longing and devotion to her still even though it had been over twenty years since her death. He never remarried after her death and raised Austin with the help of Velma. I could see why Austin wanted to care for him and make him as comfortable as possible as he aged. He didn't leave his father or send him to a nursing home. He was caring for him, spending time with him, and making sure he had all his needs met physically, mentally, and spiritually which made me love him even more.

I knew I was taking a huge risk, a chance at love…but for once in my miserable existence, I didn't care. To me, Austin was worth the risk and the challenges we faced together. Lisa was right, love *is* worth it. When you find the right one things just start falling into place as if you were meant to be together. That was certainly the case with Austin and I.

I knew leaving Tampa would not be an easy thing for me to do but let's face facts, I also now knew that I didn't want to live my life without my cowboy.